Two-Timer

by

Bali Rai

First published in 2005 in Great Britain by
Barrington Stoke Ltd, Sandeman House, Trunk's Close,
55 High Street, Edinburgh EH1 1SR
www.barringtonstoke.co.uk

ISBN 1-842993-31-3

Printed in Great Britain by Bell & Bain Ltd

A Note from the Author

When I was asked to write another book by the publisher, I decided that this time I wanted it to be fun, and a bit silly. Something that would make readers laugh. That's where the idea for *Two-Timer* came from. I was sitting, thinking about a couple of lads I knew when I was a teenager who always had more than one girl on the go, as they put it. They'd boast about it all the time. Until, that is, they got caught …

It's a very simple story, *Two-Timer*. A way of looking at the notion of karma and the old saying – "what goes around, comes around". What happens when you find yourself in a "two-girl" situation accidentally? When your mouth lets you down and you say "yes" instead of "no"? When every story you make up has to fit the last one you made up? And the next story – which you haven't even made up yet?

Like a game of chess, you've got to be a few steps ahead to survive. But it's not that easy, as Harj finds out. Enjoy!

More Bali Rai titles from
Barrington Stoke ...

Dream On

What's Your Problem?

Available to buy from our website at:

www.barringtonstoke.co.uk

Visit Bali's website at:

www.balirai.com

Many thanks to the Royal High School,
Edinburgh, who helped with the jacket for this
book, and a particular thank you to Hassan Rahman,
Sarah Heron and Iram Shafi who appeared on the
front cover.

Contents

Before We Begin ...

My dad is always saying that life is all about learning. People should try to learn something new every day. It's his motto.

"Learn for the sake of learning, innit?" he keeps on saying to me.

"Just for the hell of it?" I ask.

"Exactly, Harj, son."

"You wanna learn 'bout diets then," I say.

"Cheeky devil!" he shouts at me.

Up until about three months ago I just took no notice of him. I mean, I love him and all that but what was he going to tell me about my life? With his bald head and that fat belly that hangs over his belt, he looks like Homer Simpson but fatter and with a fart problem.

Dad didn't know what I was up to with my mates and with girls and that. He didn't have a clue. It was like that for ages.

Until three months ago that is. That was when I learned one of the first big lessons in my life. And it was the first time I understood what my dad has always said. That life is one big learning curve. It can also be one big pain in the butt. And that time it was all my fault.

I'd better tell you what happened. That's if you really want me to. I'd rather try and forget. But if you want to know and that ...

Chapter 1

Neeta

It was a boring school day, like all the others. My mates were chatting about their girlfriends and I was just listening in. The last girlfriend I'd had was when I was nine. She was called Ibiza Sunset Williams (seriously, she was). She didn't really count as a girlfriend, well, only if we were having a competition for stupid names.

We were sitting around at lunchtime – me and my best mates, Marcus, Jag and Dal. I was starting to feel the heat that comes with being 15 and still a virgin. I felt bad that I hadn't got a girl at all. My mates were talking dirty and grinning at each other.

"An' she took that ting off and out they popped," said Marcus, "like two ripe melons."

"*Yeah*?" asked Dal, looking frisky.

Marcus shook his head.

"I wish ..." he said.

"Well, *my* girl let me," said Jag. "No trouble ..."

Marcus gave him a funny look.

"*Lisa*?"

"I ain't aware of any *other* girlfriend I've got," replied Jag.

"Don't believe yer ... her parents are some of dem church goin' freaks ... no *way* she'd let you touch nuttin'," Marcus told him.

"Like you'd know," said Jag. But I saw he couldn't look Marcus in the eye.

Marcus saw too.

"*See*? You can't even look at me when you tell lies," he said.

"Kiss my arse," Jag told him and he walked off.

"No-one else is goin' to," added Dal, giggling like a girl.

I smiled. Then I began to think about having a girlfriend. Marcus must have read my mind.

"It's about time we sorted you out, Harj," he told me.

"I'm cool," I said. That was a lie.

"I seen yer checkin' out the girls when we was swimming. You never looked cool to me," said Dal.

"Least I don't piss in the pool," I told him.

Dal shook his head.

"One time, bro! When I was like *seven* ..."

"Nasty," added Marcus.

"Like yer mum," replied Dal.

"*An'* yer sister," said Marcus.

I told them I was going to the loo.
I walked away before the insults got worse.
As I turned into the corridor, I bumped into a
lad from my class, Bippin Lal. He's only been
at our school for a few months. He's just got
here from India. His dad's a computer
engineer who's just got a new job in England.

"Excuse me," he said. He's always very
polite and still has a strong Indian accent.

"No worries, bro."

He looked back at me.

"Perhaps you can tell me what you are meaning?" he said. "I do not understand the way young people speak the Queen's English in this school."

"Er ... yeah," I muttered and I tried not to grin.

"I saw Neeta at lunch," he told me.

"*Neeta?*"

"Yes – in 9MC class."

I nodded.

"Yeah – I know who she is. What about it ...?"

"She's a very *fine* young lady," said Bippin Lal.

And with that he walked off down the corridor. What a nutter! Anyway, I thought he was a nutter. What he said turned out to be a bit weird because as I went on walking down the corridor I bumped into someone else. Neeta from 9MC.

"Sorry," I muttered. I was trying hard *not* to look at her chest. Everyone did that, even the male teachers. Some of the female teachers too. "Hi, Harj!" she said with a huge smile.

I looked at her chest, looked away and then back again.

"Up *here* ..." she said and pointed at her face.

"Oh right ... yeah," I said and I looked up.

"There ... that's better," she told me.

I looked into her big brown eyes. Her face was amazing too. She was one fit girl.

"I'm goin' to this thing on Friday night and I was thinking – would you like to come with me?" she asked.

I didn't hear her. Instead, I thought I could sneak another look at her chest while she was talking – I was wrong.

"Up *here* .... yes ... *that's right*," she said with a sweet smile.

"Er ..." I stammered.

She shook her head.

"My friends said you were hard work," she went on, "but ..."

"You what?" I asked. "What friends?"

"Never mind about all that. Do you wanna go out with me or not?"

This time I heard what she said.

"*HUH*?" I replied, like a dickhead.

"Do you wanna go out with me on Friday night?"

"Er ... yeah ... yeah," I heard myself say. My heart was jumping up and down.

"Cool ..." she told me. "Here's my number."

She handed me a bit of pink paper. She'd written her mobile number on it with a purple gel pen.

"Er ... thanks," I said.

"Meet me at the gate after school," she went on. "Then you can walk me home ..."

"Er ..."

She gave me a big grin.

"Well – you can walk me back most of the way. *And* I can teach you how to speak," she added.

With that she walked off. I stood and stared after her for about five minutes. I went on staring down the corridor even after she'd gone. Other pupils walked past me, giving me funny looks. Was there something up with me? Was I like that kid who'd taken some weird pills at school once?

Then I remembered that fifteen minutes before, I'd been about two seconds away from pissing myself. I ran for the toilets as if I was my dad running after doughnuts. I made it just in time.

Back out in the corridor, I heard the bell go and walked to my lesson. As I got to the science block, I saw Mr Brimstone who was a biology teacher. He had a dog lead in his hand and at the end of it was a big grey goat.

"Mind out of the way, Harj," he said.

I looked at the goat. It looked back at me and then turned its head all the way round.

"Why have you got a goat in school, Sir?" I asked.

"Because my wife wouldn't look after it at home," said Mr Brimstone, like that made sense. He walked off and as he went, he kept on muttering under his breath.

I walked into class and sat down. All I could think about was Neeta.

Chapter 2
Kelly

The day after my first date with Neeta, I was standing in the main shopping centre in town. I watched all the people walk by. Marcus was in the Perfume Store. He wanted some cheap aftershave and he was trying to chat up the assistant behind the counter. Jag was standing next to me, yawning. Dal hadn't turned up. I was telling Jag all about my date but he wasn't interested because I hadn't "done" anything with Neeta.

"But it was a first date," I said when he told me I was a wuss.

"*So?* You could have tried something ..." he told me.

"Next time," I replied.

"That's what yer mam keeps telling yer dad," he joked.

I was fed up with his lame jokes.

"You're a dick ..." I told him.

"She's got one of them too," grinned Jag.

"What – your *sister*?"

He shook his head.

"Nope. Yer mam ..." he said.

I told him to piss off and walked into River Island to look at clothes. Jag stayed where he was. I walked upstairs and started looking at all the jeans. I'd been in there for a few minutes when someone started shouting. I turned to see who it was. A tall skinny man was arguing with a security guard and the shop manager.

14

"I was just taking it home to try on ..."

"Oh *yeah*," said the security guard. I knew him. His name was Bod and he was always trying to get us to move on when we were hanging around the shops.

"*Honest to God* ... swear on me dying mam. She's ill, man, she's really bad ..."

"Call the police," Bod told the manager.

"No, don't do that," shouted the shoplifter. "I can't go back inside ... they'll do me. I got into trouble in there before. There's guys in prison after me blood. If you call the coppers I'll go back inside. Me mam'll die and it'll be all *your* fault."

Bod yawned.

"Shut up," he said to the shoplifter. "Or I'll do you ..."

"*But* ..."

Someone tapped me on the back. I turned round. There was a girl standing behind me. A girl called Kelly who went to a different school from me. It was on the other side of town.

"Hey ... it's Harj, isn't it?" she said with a smile.

"Yeah," I said.

She lived near me and we'd gone to the same junior school.

"Ain't seen you around much," she said.

I gave a shrug. I wanted to look cool. Kelly was fit. One of the best-looking girls round where we lived. Marcus and Jag had wanted to get her phone number for ages.

"I've been about," I said.

Just then the shoplifter burst into tears and started singing really loudly.

Kelly giggled.

"He's mad," she said.

"Er ... yeah," I mumbled. I started looking at her chest.

"I was thinking," she said, "do you ... er ... do you want to maybe hang out sometime?"

Now, I *know* that I should have said no. Right there, right then. I was going out with Neeta. I shouldn't go out with Kelly too. But I was like a man coming out of the desert after weeks without water. You get my drift. So there I am, I'm staggering out of this desert and then someone throws me a bottle of ice-cold water. Am I gonna say no? Then someone gives me another bottle. What was I *meant* to do?

"Er ... yeah. That'd be cool," I said.

"Great! Shall I give you my mobile number?" she asked.

I nodded.

"How about tomorrow afternoon? Maybe we could go to the cinema or something," she said.

My heart started jumping up and down like a kangaroo on speed. I passed Kelly over my mobile and she tapped her number into it. As she walked away I smiled like a lunatic. How cool was it going to be when I told my mates about Kelly! Then my heart stopped still.

"Who was that?" asked Neeta.

There she was – behind the sale racks with another girl. Neeta looked like some kind of film star. She had this little skirt thing on and her hair was all piled up on her head.

"*Who d'you mean?*" I asked, shitting myself.

"That girl," she said.

"Oh, her ... that's Britney," I blurted out. That was the first name that came into my head.

"She doesn't go to our school," said Neeta.

"Nah – she goes to City. I know her from around."

Neeta nodded and then pulled a little top out of her bag.

"What do you think of this?" she asked.

"Er ... it's cool," I replied. *Phew!* I didn't think she'd seen Kelly with my phone.

"Do you like the colour?" Neeta went on.

I looked at the top. It was red.

"Yeah ... like red. Me favourite colour," I told her.

"Good. I'm gonna wear it for you next time we go out."

I grinned. *Two gorgeous girls to go out with!* The idea started to sink in. It felt nice.

"Great."

"Now, take me and my friend out for a coffee," Neeta said.

****

Later that night, I was sitting at home, watching my dad eat doughnuts, one after the other. The telly was on. It was the normal Saturday evening rubbish. My sister, Parvy, was on the sofa, on her phone. I picked up the remote control and pressed the text button to see what the football scores were.

"*Oi!*" shouted my dad, with his mouth full of doughnut.

"Just checkin' the footie scores," I said. "Ain't nothing on, anyway."

"Yes, there is. *I've Got No Talent, Make Me A Star*'s on ..."

"*Dad!*" shouted my sister. "Can you shut up – I'm on the phone ..."

"Who pays the bills round here?" my dad shouted back and she shut up.

"*Bollocks!*" I shouted, when I saw that my team had lost again.

"They teach you that at school?" asked my dad.

I shook my head.

"Nah – you did. That time when the plumber flooded the bathroom."

"Yeah ... well you *shouldn't* have been listening," my dad said. He sounded like a little kid.

"Oh, go and eat a doughnut, Homer."

My dad got up and grabbed the remote from me. He switched back to his programme. A fat bloke, with big glasses and wearing a dress, was singing a Britney Spears song. Well, he was trying to. I picked up my phone. Maybe I'd text Marcus. Suddenly it bleeped at me. It was Neeta. She wanted to go out tomorrow afternoon. I was about to reply and say "yes" when I remembered Kelly.

"Oh, double bollocks," I said.

"Will you stop swearing, you little shit!" my dad shouted.

"Er ... if you think about what you've just said, Dad, you'll see that you have a problem too," said my sister. She always seemed to be able to listen to five conversations at the same time. It was weird.

"And if you take a look in the mirror," replied Dad, "*you'll* see that your hair looks really weird. Who cut it? The butcher? Did you get any sausages while you were there? To go with the haircut he gave you?"

"*DAD!*" shouted my sister. I started laughing.

I was laughing so much that I'd started to cry. And then I got another message. This one was from Kelly. Could I come over to her house for midday tomorrow? Her parents were going to be out. I thought about Neeta and then about Kelly and decided that I was going to have to shift the truth around a bit. Not lie exactly. Just change the way things looked.

I'd make up a birthday party for someone in my family. How about if I said that my cousin, Onkar, was having a party tomorrow? That wasn't a proper lie. Onkar's birthday was in two months. All I was doing was moving the date a bit closer.

And that's just what I did. I sent Neeta a text telling her about Onkar's birthday. I said I'd see her at school on Monday. Then I sent Kelly a text saying I'd be at her house the next day. Neeta replied to say that it was cool and Kelly told me that she couldn't wait to see me.

After that I got myself a Coke and then sat back and watched crap telly all night long, with a big smile on my face. That's all it took. To become a two-timer.

Chapter 3

Playa Heaven

I didn't tell any of my mates for about a month. I let them think that I was only going out with Neeta. There wasn't any point in telling them the truth because I was going to have to dump one of them anyway. I just didn't know which one. And the longer I left it, the harder it got to decide.

I was having such a wicked time too. One evening I'd be out with Neeta, telling her she was my only girl and that. And the next I'd be round at Kelly's, kissing her up. It was like I had died and gone to an RnB video like them ones on *MTV*. Pure cars and gold and two girls. Playa heaven, you get me?

And it was so easy to juggle them both too. The first time that Neeta called me when I was with Kelly, I just let the phone ring and didn't answer. When I called Neeta back an hour later, I told her that I'd been doing my homework.

"So why couldn't you have answered your phone?" Neeta asked, giving me stress.

"My dad don't let me," I lied. "I ain't allowed to have my phone when I'm working."

"Oh," she replied, and she left it at that. "Well – it doesn't matter. You called me back when you could."

I grinned to myself. Then I said, "Like I wouldn't call you back, babe ... you know I'm mad for you ..."

I could hear her giggling on the other end of the line.

"*AHHH*! You're so cute," she said.

Easy. Only the next time my phone went, I was with Neeta. And this time Kelly was ringing me. When Kelly saw me next, she asked me why I hadn't answered my phone. I had to think quickly so I blurted out that someone was making joke calls to my phone. Kelly just nodded. Then she asked me if I wanted to get a DVD from the shop. It was that simple.

One Friday night, about two weeks later, I was sitting at home when Neeta rang.

"Hey," I replied, almost at once.

"Hi, babes ... I was thinking, maybe ...?" Neeta said.

"Anything for you, babe. You know that."

"Come round then ... my family have gone out to a birthday party. It's just little old me at home. *All on my lonesome ...*"

I looked at my watch. In two hours, at nine o'clock, I was meant to be going round to Kelly's for pizza and stuff. I smiled to myself as my brain worked overtime. Could I get to see Neeta before I went to Kelly's house?

"I can only come over for an hour, Neeta. My old man wants me to help him with something here."

"With what?" she asked.

"Er ... *stuff*. Boring stuff, babe ... a computer spreadsheet and that," I said without thinking.

"Oh, right."

"Do you *still* want me to come see you?" I asked, in a soft voice. A voice that I knew she liked.

"*Yeah*! My family's coming back about nine o'clock so we'd only have had a bit of time anyway."

I grinned to myself.

"On my way," I told her, and I jumped off the sofa and grabbed my jacket.

In the end I spent half an hour extra at Neeta's and by the time I left, I was rushing. I didn't have time to go home. Instead I went straight to Kelly's and turned up there, out of breath and all red in the face. She gave me a funny look when she opened the door.

"What you been doin'?" she asked.

"Nuttin'," I lied. "I was just a bit late leaving my house and I didn't want to keep you waiting so I ran."

"Just so that you'd be on time, *like you said*?" she asked, with a smile.

"Yeah – that's it," I lied again.

She leant towards me and kissed me on the cheek.

"You're so *lovely*," she told me. "I knew you'd get here on time."

I walked into the living room and looked around. Her mum wasn't home.

"Where's yer mum at?" I asked her.

"Working the late shift," she said. "It's just you and me and the sofa until at least 11 ..."

I put my arms around her and tried to kiss her like one of those old-time stars in a Hollywood movie. But Kelly pushed me back.

"What's that *smell?*" she asked me.

I could feel my face going red.

"What smell?"

"It's like someone's perfume," Kelly said.

I sniffed my arms and hands. She was right. It *was* perfume. *Neeta's* perfume.

"Oh, yeah – *that* perfume," I said, making out that it was nothing. "My sister was messing about earlier on."

"Your sister?" she asked.

I thought Kelly might work out what was really going on so I made up a story as fast as I could.

"We was watching some man on that telly programme ..." I began.

"Which one?"

"You know ... that *I've Got No Talent* thing."

Kelly looked puzzled.

"I don't watch that one," she said.

Inside I was smiling.

"There's this man on it, dressed as a woman ... messing about telling jokes ..." I said.

Kelly still didn't look as if she believed me. I went on as if I didn't care. "Anyway, this geezer dresses as a woman and my sister told me I'd look good in a dress. And *then* the mad cow went and sprayed me with her perfume."

Kelly grinned. She was looking *that* good tonight, in her tight white T-shirt and flared jeans. I looked at her chest. "It's nice perfume, whatever it is," she said.

I saw my chance, like a small door opening and I jumped.

"Don't smell half as nice as your perfume," I said, all sly like a fox.

"*Ahh* ... you're so sweet," replied Kelly, kissing me on the lips.

Sorted, just like that. No problem.

****

In the end, I told Marcus all about it. He was my oldest friend and I trusted him the most. I was going to tell Jag too but decided against it. Jag had a big mouth. And as for Dal – well, I didn't really get on too well with him anyhow. He was Jag's mate, not mine. Marcus and me were in town, on a Saturday, when I let my secret out. We were in a café, watching the girls walk by.

After I'd finished telling him, he looked at me like I was mad.

"*Get lost, Harj!*" he told me.

"Nah – I'm serious, mate."

"*Kelly* Kelly? The fit one that goes to City?"

I nodded.

"Nah – you're *lyin'*, man. Ain't no *way* you've got her on the go an' all. It's bad enough that an ugly bwoi like you is going out with Neeta. Talk about beauty and the beast."

I shook my head at him.

"Why would I lie about it?" I asked.

"To big yourself up, man," he replied.

"But I don't want to big myself ..."

"Yeah, you do. That's what we *all* do, you get me? We *compete*," he added.

"Not me," I told him.

"*What* – so first you ain't got no girl and now you have two – *just like that*? And you're not lying to make yourself look good?" he asked.

"No – I ain't."

"Well – I don't believe you, Harj. *Prove it.*"

I sighed and took my mobile out. I knew Marcus would get a shock. Like maybe he'd slap me on the back or call me sly or something. But I never thought he wouldn't believe me. I went into my text message inbox and found a load of texts from Kelly. I handed him my mobile.

"Here – read these if you don't believe me," I told him.

Marcus grabbed the phone and started to look through the texts. He didn't say anything until he'd checked them all out. Then he whistled softly.

"You ain't lying, are you?" he said.

"I told you, man ..."

He scratched his head.

"So, tell me, Mr Loverman, how d'you end up with *two* girls?"

I didn't know what to tell him. I mean, it's not like I'd planned it. I hadn't spent ages chasing either of them. They'd just come to me, and all in the same week.

"Just lucky, I guess," I replied.

"*Lucky?* You're telling me ... Both fit girls an' all ..."

I looked at him.

"Just one of them things, bro," I told him. "Both of them came on to me. I was shocked. That's why I couldn't say no to Kelly, you get me?"

Marcus shook his head and started to laugh.

"You just *couldn't* say no ..." he said to me. He was laughing at me now. "You was all *confused*. Nuttin' to do with the fact that you got greedy ..."

"I swear – it weren't like that ..." I went on.

"So what you gonna do now?" he asked.

"I dunno. Drop one of them, I guess ..."

Marcus grinned.

"Yeah, but *which* one?" he asked. "It's like giving up diamond for pearl, you get me?"

I did get him. How was I going to decide which one to drop? One of them had to go. I knew one day I'd get caught out. I mean, even at that point, when I was juggling things like an expert, I *knew* my luck couldn't last. Even so – knowing what you *should* do and then *doing* it are two different things.

Chapter 4
Too Easy

Marcus didn't say a word to Dal and Jag. I made him promise. But that didn't stop him from giving me a hard time every time we were on our own. He even did it in front of Neeta once but she didn't understand him.

He came up to Neeta and me in the school dinner hall. "Hey, man, look at you!" he said. "So greedy for girls."

When Neeta had gone, I turned to Marcus. "That was too close for comfort," I said. "You trying to get me killed or what?"

But all he did was grin.

"Can't stand the heat, rude boy, leave the jugglin' to someone else."

"But ..." I began.

"Two-timer," said Marcus.

"SSSHH!"

"Leave it out ... no-one heard," he grinned. "You need to relax, bro."

"Easy for you to say," I replied.

"No, it's you it's easy for, boy. With yer two fine gal."

I told him to get lost and walked off on my own.

But his teasing didn't stop me. I just carried on with my games. I told more lies on top of the lies I'd told already. In the end even I had trouble remembering what I'd said.

One night I was with Neeta, in Burger King. We'd been to a movie and I'd gone to get some food. I came back with a chicken burger for her because it was her favourite. Only it wasn't. That was what Kelly liked best.

"What you got me that for?" she asked. "It smells."

"It's your fav ..." I began. I had to work out what I needed to say quickly. "It's your *fault* ... your fault. You didn't tell me what you wanted," I spat out.

Neeta picked up a chip and threw it at me.

"You never asked me," she pointed out. "You just went marching over to the counter like a big macho man ..."

The only thing to do was to say "sorry". It always helped.

"Sorry," I said to her. My voice went all soft and sheepish.

She smiled.

"It's OK ... I don't mind it when you do stuff without asking me ... I feel all girlie," she said.

"Er ... yeah," I told her. "So do you want something else?"

"No, I'll just swap with you," she said. "You have my chicken burger. You've spent plenty of money on me already today ..."

She was right too. But every day was the same. She never spent any of *her* money.

Neeta grabbed my burger and started eating it. *Should I drop her because she was so tight with her money?* I asked myself.

But then my eyes started to move down to her chest again and I changed my mind.

"Er ... you getting a good look?" she asked with a grin.

"I just want to read what it says on your ..." I began to say.

"Yeah ... of course you do. Wanna touch them?"

"Huh?" I said. I was shocked. So shocked that I dropped the bag of fries I was holding.

"Just kidding ..." she smiled sweetly.

My eyes started moving down again, as if they were made of iron and her breasts were magnets.

"You read slowly, don't you?" Neeta said with a laugh.

I looked at her and started to grin.

"Yeah ... that writing's too small. I can't see it properly."

"No ..." she said slowly. "You're just an idiot. But you're my idiot, so that's fine ..."

Two days later I was sitting on Kelly's sofa. She was going to put a DVD in the machine.

"It's your birthday soon, innit?" I said to her.

"Er ..."

"February 14th – Valentine's Day."

"No, my birthday's in June," she told me.

"Oh, yeah – that's right," I said, cussing myself. It was Neeta's birthday that was on Valentine's Day.

Kelly came and sat back down on the sofa. She looked at me, puzzled. "It's a funny thing to get wrong," she told me. "Valentine's Day and June are miles apart."

I gave a shrug.

"I'm tired from footie," I lied. "I was thinking about Valentine's Day and I got all mixed up somehow ..."

What was I saying? It sounded like rubbish.

"Do you know someone whose birthday *is* the same day as Valentine's?" she asked.

"Er ... yeah ... me mum," I said.

Kelly gave me another funny look.

"Now I know that you must be tired," she said.

"Huh?" I asked. What had I said wrong now?

"You said your mum's birthday was in November."

"Nah ..." I began.

Kelly punched my arm.

"Yes, you did. You told me that night when we went to see the fireworks," she reminded me.

"Yeah, well," I began, "the thing is, my mum was adopted. She was an orphan and when her parents took her they didn't know when her birthday was so they gave her one in November ..."

Kelly looked at me. I could see she didn't believe my story.

"You what?"

"Yeah ... but after that, they did some tests on her ... you know to find out how old she was and that and that's when they found out that she was born in February."

"Really?" asked Kelly.

I nodded. I was amazed at what had just come out of my mouth. What would happen if Kelly met my family and asked them? Now I had to do something to cover my tracks, so that Kelly would never ask them.

"It's like this big family secret thing, Kel."

"That's such a lovely story," she said. She believed every word now.

"Just don't ever tell anyone I told you," I begged. "My dad'll kill me and my mum will be really upset."

Kelly put her hand on my arm.

"I won't tell anyone," she said.

"I shouldn't have said anything," I added. I'd started another set of lies as if they were a cheap aftershave. Enough of them and you couldn't smell the first lie I'd told.

"I promise," she said. "I'll never tell them."

I looked away. I knew this time I'd had a very narrow escape.

That night, when I got home, I made a promise to myself. I was going to stop telling such big lies. But it didn't work. The longer I kept going out with Neeta *and* Kelly, the more lies I had to tell. After a while, it was like a game. I wanted to see what I could get away with. I know it sounds bad now but back then I was stuck and I carried on lying because I didn't know what else to do.

Chapter 5
Happy Valentine's?

It started to go wrong around Valentine's Day. It was a Friday and I'd been invited to a party with Neeta. Rachel Boon, a girl in Year 10, was giving the party. Her parents were away and she'd invited loads of people. I was in a good mood. It was Neeta's birthday (remember?!) and she'd liked the presents I'd given her.

By the time we got to Rachel's house, we were both a bit pissed. Mitesh, who was Neeta's big brother, had given her some alcopops and we'd both drunk a few. Mitesh

was coming to Rachel's party too, later on.
I knew him from school but I didn't like him.
He was in Year 10, in the same class as
Rachel. He was big and ugly. He thought he
was the best and everyone was too scared to
tell him different.

Rachel's house was full of people and
there was loud music playing.

I left Neeta with two of her friends and
went to look round the house. It was huge.
There were about ten rooms downstairs and
even more upstairs. There were people
everywhere. I went out into the garden
where some lads I knew were having a smoke.
I had a chat with them and a cigarette. Then
I went back inside. In the massive kitchen I
saw Marcus kissing up his girlfriend, Sunny.
As I passed by I poked him and he let go of
her to see who it was.

"Easy, *loverbwoi*!" he grinned.

"Leave it out, bro," I told him.

Sunny went off to get a drink. Marcus turned to me.

"What you gonna do then?" he asked me.

"About what?" I asked.

"The two-timer thing, bro."

I gave a shrug.

"Can't do much tonight, can I?" I replied. I could hear some girls giggling by the kitchen door.

Marcus grinned. It was a smile that said he knew something I didn't.

"*What is it?*" I asked him. What did he know?

"Is Neeta here?" he said, still grinning.

"Yeah ... *why?*" I wanted to know what he was on about.

"Er ... best I just let you find out," said Marcus. He looked down at the floor as if there was someone nearby that he didn't want to see.

I turned around and nearly farted. It was Kelly.

"*Hi!*" she gave me a huge grin, then she grabbed me and pulled me close to her.

Her breath smelt of booze and her eyes were all misty. She was drunk.

"Wh-wha-what you doin' here?" I stammered, looking around to make sure Neeta wasn't in the kitchen too.

"Rachel invited me," Kelly replied. She looked hurt. "*Why?*"

"We were gonna go out tomorrow," I said.

"Yeah, I *know* that!" she giggled. "It's just that Rachel's an old friend and she *asked* me and I said *yes*."

I gulped down air. I needed to do some serious juggling or else I'd be a dead man.

"So *this* is the party you said you were going to?" she asked me.

"Er ... yeah ..." I replied.

"You said you had to go to a party with your sister because she's all alone on Valentine's," mumbled Kelly.

She looked at Marcus and gave him a drunken grin.

"Harj is *so-oh* lovely," she told him. "Look at him – he gives up his Valentine's night to be with his sister because she's just split up with her boyfriend."

Marcus gave me a look. Then he said to Kelly, "You know Harj," and he smiled, "he's a real softy."

Kelly burped.

"*Oops*! Sorry about that."

I glared at Marcus.

"I love boys who have feelings," said Kelly, and she pinched my arse.

"Oh, you wouldn't *believe* how much Harj cares about stuff," Marcus went on. "He's like a *saint*."

"I hope not," said Kelly, with a wink at me.

I just stood where I was for a moment. I couldn't move. Then I thought of something to do.

"Come on, babe," I said to Kelly. "Let's go outside and have a chat."

Marcus cracked up laughing.

"Romantic walk in the moonlight," he croaked.

"*Piss off*!" I whispered.

Kelly took my hand and pulled me along behind her. I looked around, making sure no-one saw us.

I got back to meet up with Neeta about 15 minutes later. I left Kelly in the kitchen. She'd met up with some of her friends from school. She was getting really drunk now and part of me hoped that she'd pass out or something. Then she'd have to go home. But she just kept going. Neeta was in one of the front rooms, where the music system was. She gave me a filthy look when I came in.

"Where have you *been*?" she spat. "I got all my friends here and you go running off to see your mates."

"Sorry – I seen Marcus," I told her.

"What were you doing – *snogging* him?" she asked, and laughed in a horrid, sneering way.

"Just chatting," I said with a shrug. "Sorry ..."

I met some of the girls she was with. I nodded and said "yes" at the right times as they chatted on to me. I wanted to get out of there fast. I looked around and saw a few people I knew. But most of the people were Rachel's friends. Posh kids like Neeta. They didn't know me. That was cool with me. If no-one knew me, I might not get caught out. All I had to do was keep my two girlfriends apart. For the next five hours.

That was what did it in the end. I wanted to challenge myself. See if I could do it. It turned into a game and that was why it went wrong. I should have just left then. Pretended I was ill or something. Maybe gone and hid. Or taken the next flight to Mars. But no, not me. Stupid, big-head, idiot me thought I'd have a laugh. As if ...

I spent 20 minutes with Neeta and her friends and then I told her that I had to go to the toilet.

"Try and get back before next year," she said and winked at me.

The room we were in had three doors to it. I took the one that led back to the kitchen. It was time to find Kelly again.

She was still in the kitchen with her friends. When she saw me, she grabbed hold of me and kissed me a load of times. She looked amazing, in a little dress and with her hair up. I looked around. There was no-one who knew me anywhere close, so I kissed her back. Her friends giggled.

"He's *gorgeous*," Kelly told them. "Aren't you, Harj?"

"Er ... if you say so," I replied.

"Don't be shy now," I heard a voice I knew say behind me. It was Jag.

I looked at him and shook my head just a little bit. Enough for him to see.

"Summat wrong with your head, bro?" he asked.

I let Kelly go.

"I've just gotta talk to Jag," I told her. "Won't be a minute."

She smiled at me then she burped again.

"*Oops*!" she giggled. "Keep doing that."

"I'll be back in two minutes," I said.

"*Anything for my boyfriend*," she replied as if she was in a movie.

I grabbed Jag and dragged him out into the garden.

"Easy, Harj!"

"Just mind your own business," I told him.

"I was," he said. "I didn't expect to see you kissing up no other girl. That one said you were her boyfriend. Where's Neeta?"

I didn't say anything.

"You playin' Neeta?" he asked.

I nodded. I thought he'd slag me off but he didn't. Instead he slapped me on the back and grinned.

"Yes, Harj!"

"Keep it down, man," I replied. Inside I was dead pleased with how he'd taken my news.

"I didn't know you had it in you. She's fit an' all ... you wanna ditch that Neeta."

I looked down.

"I'm serious, man. Neeta ain't nuttin' compared to her," he went on.

"Just leave it, Jag," I told him.

"Whatever you say, loverbwoi," he replied. He was grinning like a madman.

I left him where he was and went back to find Kelly. But when I got back to the kitchen she'd gone. One of her friends was still there.

"Where's Kelly gone?" I asked her.

"Upstairs," replied her friend. "She said you should go and find her."

Her friend winked. I thanked her and then I went back to find Neeta.

Chapter 6
Mitesh

When I got back into the main room, Neeta had gone too. It was dark in there and I walked around to try and find her but it was no good. She wasn't there.

I went back out into the hallway. I walked past a load of people getting off with each other and had to be careful not to step into a pool of sick. From somewhere in the house I heard a crash, glass breaking and then a scream. How was Rachel going to explain it all to her parents? I didn't really care. I had my own problems. What if Neeta had seen me with Kelly or someone had told her?

Neeta had to be somewhere. If I started looking for her at the front of the house and then worked my way back to the garden I'd have to find her.

I began to search each room. In the third room I tried, there were two Year 11s on a sofa. I span round and walked out quickly. I wasn't enjoying this party much! By the time I'd gone into all the downstairs rooms and was in the garden again, I still hadn't seen Neeta. I walked past Meena Smith, a girl from my year. I knew she was pregnant but there she was, snogging someone who wasn't her boyfriend. I shook my head. I needed to get some fresh air. Then I'd go and look upstairs. My head was spinning and I wanted to sit down.

I found an iron bench, like the ones that you get in parks, and I sat down. As I did, a naked lad ran past, holding a candle. I shook my head again. Where had Neeta gone? I heard someone laughing behind me. It was the naked lad, Martin Broad. He had lit the candle. Now he was limbo dancing and letting the wax drip onto his chest. A load of his mates and some girls were egging him on. Lunatics. I turned back round, just as someone grabbed at my collar.

"What the ...?" I began.

"Shut up!" shouted Mitesh, Neeta's older brother.

I looked at him and gave him a big smile. Was he having a laugh at Martin and his mates too?

"Easy, Mitesh ..." I said. He had grabbed my collar a bit too hard.

He didn't let go. Instead he pulled me up to his face.

"I seen you," he whispered. His voice sounded evil.

"Huh?" I asked.

"Don't pretend you don't know."

"I don't know what you're on about," I said, lying. I knew just what he meant. He'd seen me with Kelly.

"If you don't tell me the truth, I'm gonna batter you," he said. And he looked right into my eyes.

I looked away.

"Look ... it ... it's not what it seems, OK?"

"So that *wasn't* you that I saw, grabbing up some other girl's arse and snogging her ...?"

I nodded.

"It was – but she just jumped on me," I lied. "I was trying to get her to stop but she's a *nutter*. She's been following me round for days."

"I don't believe you," he said. He spat all over me as he spoke.

I badly wanted to wipe my face but he was still holding me and he was a big lad.

"Honest ... I was gonna tell Neeta – just not tonight. That girl, Kelly, she's been hassling me for *weeks*. She's even turned up at my house and all."

Mitesh looked at me and then let go. I wiped my face with my hand and went on blagging.

"She's a nutter. I mean – I don't even *like* the girl ..."

"Really?" asked Mitesh.

"I'm goin' out with your sister, bro ..."

"So you don't mind if I get off with her?"

"Who – yer sister?" I asked, like a twerp.

Mitesh slapped me like I was a little kid.

"I meant that Kelly," he snapped.

"Yeah – sorry ... I'm a bit drunk," I told him.

"You'll be a bit *dead* if I don't get to meet that girl tonight," Mitesh told me.

"Huh?"

Mitesh grinned at me. He looked like an evil madman in a spy film. You know the kind that always have fat white cats and plan to destroy the world.

"If you don't make *sure* I get off with Kelly, I'm gonna tell Neeta all about you. And after that, I'll kill you ..." he told me. He was still smiling.

I took some deep, deep breaths. I needed them. My secret life as a two-timer was coming to an end. A messy, slapped in the face, beaten to a pulp type of end. I tried to think of a way out but it was no good. I was dead meat, one way or another. I mean, how could I get Kelly to snog Mitesh? I couldn't

65

take him up to her and go, "Hey, Kel, this is my *other* girl's brother. He wants to get into your *bra* – think you could *help* me out here?" I was a goner.

"*Well?*" asked Mitesh.

"Well what?" I replied. "I mean I'll go and find Kelly and you two can meet but if she don't like you, then what can I do?"

"You saying I'm ugly or something?" he said.

"Nah, bro. Nuttin' like that. It's just not that simple, is it?"

The madman smile came back.

"It better be," Mitesh told me. "For your sake."

I shrugged.

"OK – I'll do my best," I told him.

"You got ten minutes," Mitesh said. "I'm just going to check on my girlfriend then I'll meet you by the stairs."

I nodded. Well, what else could I do? I sat back down on the bench and watched Mitesh walk away. My brain was working hard. I needed to find a way out. But it was no good. I felt like I was going to be shot. I just had to wait for the bullet.

After about five minutes I walked back into the house. In the kitchen I saw Marcus chatting up some girls.

"Bro – I need your help," I told him. He was bragging about how fast he could run to the group of girls.

"I'm in the middle of a something here," he replied.

"Bro!"

"OK, man! Ladies, do excuse my friend. He seems to have his knickers in a bit of a twist," he said.

The girls looked at me and giggled. I didn't care. I was too worried. I grabbed Marcus and pulled him to one side, and away from a really sick looking Year 10 lad.

"What's the big deal?" Marcus asked me.

"I got trouble," I told him.

"What – someone having a go at you?"

I nodded.

"Yeah – Neeta's brother."

Marcus looked at me.

"Oh yeah?" he asked.

I told him everything that Mitesh had said to me. Marcus listened and nodded as I spoke. When I'd finished he shook his head.

"I dunno what I can do," he told me. "You're gonna have to deal with it, bro."

"But he wants me to make sure Kelly fancies him," I croaked.

"May as well try to make it rain," Marcus said. "That Mitesh is so ugly when he was born the doctor slapped his mum, you get me?"

"This ain't no time for lame jokes," I said. "I'm a dead man."

"If it gets too hot, you gotta stay out of the kitchen, bro," he told me.

"Anything else useful to tell me?" I said. I didn't want any more jokes.

Marcus gave a shrug.

"Come on then," he said. "I'll help you out. Where's Kelly?"

"Upstairs somewhere," I told him.

"And Mitesh?"

"Waiting by the stairs for me," I replied.

"Best go try and sort this then," Marcus said.

"How?" I asked him.

He shrugged again.

"I ain't got a clue," he admitted.

Chapter 7
Blind (Drunk) Date

Mitesh gave me and Marcus a funny look when we got to him.

"It takes *both* of you?" he asked, with a horrid smile.

"We gotta *find* her," I told him. "Marcus said he'd help."

"Whatever ..." said Mitesh. "Just get on with it."

"Why don't you chill here and when we find her, one of us will come and get you?" Marcus put in.

I nodded.

"Yeah – no point you having to trek around this massive house looking for her. She might have gone home by now, anyway ..."

Mitesh smiled again.

"She'd better not have ..." he warned. "I'll be right here. *Waiting*."

I followed Marcus up the stairs. At the top, the stairs went two ways. Then there were some more stairs, up to another floor.

"Man – what do Rachel's parents do for money?" asked Marcus, with a whistle.

"It's big, innit."

"Like one of them pop star pads," he said.

"You go left," I said, "and I'll go right."

He nodded and walked off. There were ten bedrooms to check out, as well as four bathrooms and two toilets. And there were people everywhere. And I mean everywhere.

The first bedroom I checked was piled high with coats. I couldn't even see the bed. There were about 30 people in the second room. That one had Rachel's name on the door. They were sitting all over the place, drinking and snogging and stuff. I saw Rachel and asked her if she had seen Neeta but she shook her head. I thought about asking if she'd seen Kelly too but I changed my mind. *Not a good move*, I thought.

Next to Rachel's room was a bathroom, which was locked. I stood and listened at the door but I couldn't hear anything. I left it and walked into another bedroom. A strong, sweet smell hit my nostrils as I opened the door. The room was full of lads. A few of them hid stuff behind their backs as I stuck my head through the door.

"What do you want?" asked one of them.

They were Year 11 rugby players so I said sorry and shut the door. I was in enough trouble. I didn't need to get kicked in by the rugby team too. I stepped over two girls who were lying on the floor, giggling.

"Come and lie down," one of them said to me.

"Yeah – it's cool down here," said the other one.

"I'm looking for someone," I told them. "A girl called Kelly."

"Kelly with the dark hair?" asked one of the girls.

"Yeah … you seen her?" I asked.

The girl lifted her hand and pointed back over her head.

"She's in the room right at the end," she told me. "She's pissed."

The girls giggled.

"Thanks," I replied. I walked past another bedroom and bathroom and went right up to the last door.

As I got to it, I heard more giggling and I knocked. One of Kelly's friends came to the door. She smiled and turned round to Kelly.

"He's *here*!" she said. Then she giggled some more.

I walked into the room and nearly had a heart attack. Kelly and her friends were lying on a massive bed. They were all whispering to each other.

"*What you doin'*?" I asked Kelly.

She got up and walked over to me. Even when I was in real trouble, with death and disaster just round the corner, I couldn't help looking at her chest.

"Up *here*!" she giggled. "God – he's *always* looking at my tits," she told her friends.

They started to have giggling fits.

"This looks like Rachel's parents' room," I told her.

She smiled in a dreamy sort of way.

"It *is*," she said. "We've just been trying on her mum's clothes."

"What – are you crazy?" I asked her.

Kelly burped, said sorry and then nodded.

"Well, *you* didn't turn up," she said slowly. She couldn't talk properly any more. "What's a girl gonna do?"

I told her to put Rachel's mum's clothes away and tried to think of a way to get her to agree to meeting Mitesh. In the end, as her friends got off the bed, I just lied. Again. I was still lying when Marcus came in.

"Looks like I missed the best party," he said, looking at Kelly's three friends.

"We can always have another party ..." one of the girls said with a snigger.

Marcus nodded slowly.

"*No, you can't!*" I said.

76

"Spoilsport," he said, with a grin.

"She's out of it," I said to Marcus. Kelly was swaying to and fro.

"That's OK then," replied Marcus. "She won't see that Mitesh hit every branch on his way down the ugly tree."

I shook my head.

"I don't feel right about this," I told him, in a whisper. "I mean – I really like her, you get me?"

Marcus shook his head too.

"Well, what was all that jugglin' about then?" he asked.

"Who's jugglin'?" asked Kelly. She really did sound drunk now. "Is there a *clown*? I *love* clowns."

"What you wanna do, bro?" asked Marcus. "Run now or run later?"

I put my hands in my pockets.

Kelly hugged me to her.

"Ahhh ... has my baby boy got problems?" she said.

"Er ..." I began.

"So where's this cousin you want me to meet?" she asked.

"He's not a *real* cousin," I continued to lie. "He's like a friend of my cousin's but he wanted to meet you."

Kelly pointed to herself and fell sideways onto the bed. Her friends started laughing again.

"Liddle old me?" Kelly asked. "Is he as *gorgeous* as you?"

"Er ... he's a bit different," I told her. *Different* like a being from another planet.

"Can I *snog* him, then?" she asked. She tried to get up off the bed.

I could see that she was out of her tree and I felt bad about setting her up with Mitesh. I had told lies and cheated, but what I was doing now was even worse. Only I didn't have a choice. And, anyway, maybe she wouldn't get off with him. There was a knock at the door. I went over and opened it, just a bit. It was Mitesh.

"She in there?" he asked, with a grin.

"Yeah – but she's pissed up, man," I said. I wished I could put him off.

Mitesh pushed the door into my face and walked in. I turned and looked at Kelly.

"Er ... Kelly – this is my cousin. The one I told you about."

Mitesh looked at me and smiled.

"Yeah," he said, "I'm the good-looking member of the family."

Kelly peered at him. Her friends started giggling even more. Girls are amazing. It's like they've got giggles in a bottle and they can pour some out anytime they want.

"Leave me to it," whispered Mitesh.

"Huh?" I asked.

"*Get out the room before I break your legs*," he snapped.

I looked at Kelly.

"I'll be back in a bit," I told her.

She burped, said sorry and then smiled at me.

"OK," she said. Then she fell over again, back on to the bed.

I walked out. I felt sick and looked at Marcus.

"Come on," I said, "let's go."

Marcus shook his head.

"Not me, bro. I'm gonna listen in. Kelly's gonna tell him to get lost," he told me.

"So I just stand here and wait for him to batter me?" I asked.

Marcus opened the door. There were some shouts and laughs. He grinned.

"If I was you," he said. "I'd do a runner right now ..."

I was about to ask him what he meant when I heard Kelly yelling at Mitesh.

"... You look like a *gorilla*," I heard her say. "Did your mummy *cry* when you were born ..."

I gulped down air. I was a dead man.

"... Cos if she didn't she must be *blind*," Kelly went on.

I looked at Marcus who was trying not to laugh out loud. He had tears pouring down his cheeks.

"I'll call you on your mobile in ten minutes," I told him.

Then I turned and ran before Mitesh could get hold of me.

Chapter 8
Truth Hurts

As I left the party, I looked for Neeta one
last time. But she had gone. I looked
everywhere, but I had to try and hide from
Mitesh at the same time. In the end I jumped
over Rachel's fence and hid in the next-door
driveway. I watched Mitesh and two of his
mates leave. He looked well angry and was
cussing me as he left. At one point he was
just on the other side of the fence to me, and
I could hear him tell his mates that he was
going to batter me when he got hold of me.
I waited until he'd gone. Then I rang Marcus
on his mobile.

Five minutes later, Marcus came out of the house with Kelly. She was still smiling and swaying to and fro. I took her hand and told her that I would take her home. Marcus walked most of the way with us, as he only lived round the corner from me. We took Kelly back first and then, when he turned into his street, I told him that I'd ring him the next day.

"You wanna be careful," he told me. "Mitesh was well mad. He's gonna tell Neeta for sure ..."

"I don't care anymore," I told him. "She's an idiot anyway."

"You're in for some grief, you know that," he added.

"Yeah – I know," I said. "I deserve it ..."

Marcus shook his head.

"No-one deserves to get beaten up," he said. "And that's what's gonna happen when Mitesh sees you."

"It's weird," I replied, "but when I saw Mitesh and Kelly together, I saw how much I liked her."

Marcus grinned.

"You're a nutter," he said. Then he walked off.

I spent the next day trying to ring Neeta. I'd made up my mind to try and tell her about Kelly before her brother did. Knowing my luck, he'd already told her. She wasn't answering her mobile or her house phone, so I thought Mitesh must have told her. But that didn't stop me from trying to ring. I tried to ring Kelly too. I didn't want us to finish with her mad at me. Her mum told me that she was in bed with a bad head.

"Did she have a bit to drink last night?" her mum asked.

"Erm ... I dunno," I lied.

"It's OK, Harj. I don't mind her having a drink. Just not that much. She looks awful. I've been worried about her."

"She'll be OK," I said.

"I expect so. See you soon," her mum replied.

"I hope so," I told her. And I did hope I'd see Kelly and her mum again.

I thought I was going to lose both my girlfriends. I didn't care about Neeta. I was fed up with her anyway, and I didn't like the way that she'd talked to me at the party.

But I didn't want Kelly to find out about Neeta. I wanted to try and stay with Kelly.

That evening, my dad was watching *I've Got No Talent* again. This time he was eating

86

biscuits from a tin. I sat down next to him and gave a huge sigh.

"What's up with you?" he asked. He kept on looking at the telly and didn't look at me.

"Girl trouble," I said.

"Girls are all trouble," he told me. "Look at your sister."

"I'm being serious, Dad."

He put the tin of biscuits on the coffee table. Now he turned to look at me.

"If you're about to tell me that I'm going to be a grandfather, I'll whip you so bad ..." he warned.

"Nuttin' like that, man. I just messed up, that's all," I told him

"How?" he asked.

"Do you really care?" I asked.

He gave me a big grin. "Try me, bub."

So I told him everything, from day one. My dad sat and listened and didn't butt in once. When I was done, he just shook his head.

"You've got some bottle," he told me.

I looked at him. I didn't know what he meant.

"When I was your age," he went on, "we never even had girlfriends. My old man would have beat me ... and look at you now. You've got two of them."

I gave a long sigh.

"Not any more," I said.

"Well, that's what you get for messing about with them," he told me. "Serves you right."

"I know that, Dad. I don't need a lecture," I moaned.

"Nah – just a good kicking," he said with a grin.

"Well, I'm gonna get one of them on Monday at school," I told him.

"You made your bed," he replied, "you gotta lie in it now."

"Yeah, but ..." I began to say.

"Yeah but nothing."

I grabbed a biscuit from the tin and looked at it.

"If you ain't going to eat that, put it back," my dad said. He looked at the chocolate finger I was holding. "It's my favourite."

I threw the biscuit back in the tin. My dad picked it up, looked at it as if it was a child that someone had hurt, and then ate it.

"What am I gonna do about Kelly?" I said.

My dad shrugged.

"Tell her the truth, you little rat," he said, with a smile.

"*Dad*!"

"I'm serious, Harj. Bite the bullet and tell her before someone else does."

I shook my head at him.

"Oh yeah," I said. "Shall I just ring her up and say, 'Hey, I really like you but I've been cheating on you from day one? Will that do the trick?"

"Would you rather she found out from someone else?" Dad asked me.

"But ..."

"You made the mess, Harj. Now be a man and fix it ..."

"I don't know how to ..."

My dad smiled.

"Learn as you go, bub."

"But ..." I began to protest.

"No 'buts', Harj. It's the only way," he told me. Then he got up.

"I'm off down the pub," he said.

"*Great* ..." I replied.

"Just try and ring," Dad said firmly.

"She ain't picking up her phone."

He shook his head.

"You kids," he said, "you just don't have a clue. If she ain't picking up her phone – just go round and see her. Take some flowers. Maybe a crash helmet, too."

Then he walked out of the room. He was laughing to himself about the joke he'd made. Mocking me!

I didn't do what my dad said. I didn't go round to Kelly's. But the next day I did try and ring her and Neeta over and over again.

I left a load of messages too. Neither of them called back. In the evening I went round to see Kelly like Dad had said. No-one came to the door and all the lights were off. So I went to see Marcus and chilled with him until about nine in the evening. Then I walked home and went up to my room.

I played on my PlayStation until I was too tired to play any more. As I lay on my bed, I knew that the next morning, Monday, I was going to get loads of grief. But my dad had been right about one thing. I had made the mess, and I couldn't get out of it now, no matter how bad or sorry I felt. So much for all that juggling.

So much for being a two-timer.

Chapter 9
Played?

At school the next day I didn't even get to lunchtime without a fight. Mitesh came to find me in the toilets during morning break. I was washing my hands when he walked in. I saw him in the mirror. He was with two mates. Everyone else went out and those two stood guard on the door. My stomach turned over as I waited for Mitesh to beat me up.

"You think you're clever?" he asked me, as I turned to face him.

I couldn't think of what to say.

"Nuttin' I say is gonna make a difference," I told him. "Just get on with it."

"Bad boy, hey?" he asked, with a smirk.

"Least I don't look like a gorilla," I said. That was a stupid thing to say, I know.

Mitesh head-butted me. My nose began to throb and bleed. Then he smacked me in the mouth a couple of times. After that, his mates hit me too. The last thing I heard Mitesh say was, "Be thankful I ain't told my sister yet."

That was what I was thinking about when I passed out.

Just before lunch I opened my eyes and remembered what had happened to me. I was in one of the toilet cubicles and the door was locked. My arms were wrapped round the bottom of the toilet. I groaned and turned over. There, in the same toilet, was the goat that Mr Brimstone had brought to school. I *think* it was the same goat. I don't really know about goats but in my school the weirdest stuff happens all the time. Maybe someone else had a pet goat too. I got up and pushed the goat to one side. Then I unlocked the door. The goat pushed me back with its head a few times then it started to drink from the toilet bowl. I left it where it was and walked over to the mirror.

I looked like Mitesh. Ape-like. My nose was swollen and my eyes were black. One of my cheeks was swollen too and I had a big gash above my left eye. I gave a cough and spat out blood from the back of my throat. Then I turned on the tap and splashed my face with cold water. It made my face burn a bit less. I cleaned up the blood with toilet paper. Now what should I do? I wasn't going to tell the teachers about Mitesh. You didn't do that at my school. And it was my fault I'd got beaten up. I had cheated on his sister. I would have been just as mad if someone had done that to my sister.

I stood and looked at myself for about ten minutes. Other pupils came in and out of the toilets and they all sniggered when they saw my face. I didn't care. In the end, I went to find my mates and tell them that I was going home. My head was killing me. I turned round. What had happened to the goat? Maybe I had dreamt it all. What did it matter anyway? I walked out of the toilets and went to the dinner hall.

I was just outside the hall when I got stopped by a teacher. She was so upset when she saw my face. She started fussing and flapping over me.

"What happened to you, Harjinder?" she asked me over and over again.

"Nuttin'," I replied about six times.

"Was it someone at school?"

I shook my head.

"I got beat up on the way to school,"
I lied.

"*Oh my God*!" she yelled. "Wait here – I'm going to get Mrs Pincher."

Mrs Pincher was the head. There was no way I was going to wait for her. As soon as the teacher had gone, I made my way into the dinner hall, and walked right up to Marcus and Dal.

"What the *hell* happened to your face?" asked Dal.

"Mitesh," I said.

Marcus shook his head.

"I'm gonna *get* him," he said. "My mate doesn't deserve that bad a beating."

"You seen Neeta?" I asked as if I hadn't heard what he'd said.

Marcus looked at Dal and then down to the floor. He knew something I didn't.

"*What?*" I said.

"About that Neeta ..." he began. I stopped listening.

I'd turned round and now I could see what he was about to tell me. Neeta was standing with two of her friends, and she was holding hands with another lad. Jag. I looked back at Marcus.

"That man's a *snake*," he said. "He told her about you at the party. That's why she left ..."

"She left with Jag," added Dal.

"I thought he was going out with Lisa?" I asked.

Dal shook his head.

"That was all a blag. He's been seeing Neeta for about three weeks," he told me.

I felt as if someone had punched me in the stomach – again. And then I started to get angry. I thought I was a player but now I was the person getting played. I turned and looked over at Neeta again.

"Whatever happened to your face?" I heard someone with an Indian accent ask. It was Bippin Lal. I looked at him.

"Nuttin'," I lied.

"But you look like you have been badly hurt," replied Bippin Lal. His face was upset.

"Well done. You noticed," I said. I wished that he would get lost.

I turned round to speak to Marcus again. Just then someone tapped me on the back.

"Bippin Lal – will you get ..." I began to say. Only it wasn't him. It was Neeta.

She looked at me for a few moments and then she slapped my face. It hurt so badly, I bent over and put my hands over my face. That was when I felt the water. Someone poured a jug of cold water all over my head. I stood up. I was soaked. Then the whole dinner hall started laughing. Only Marcus and Dal were silent.

"Look, bro," began Marcus, but I didn't wait to hear him. I just ran.

I walked back home slowly. The school was about three miles from my house and it took me nearly an hour to get near home.

I turned into Kelly's street. What would she think if she saw me? In that odd way that things happen in life, as I went past her house, she came out.

I looked at her and then looked the other way.

"What happened to *you*?" she asked.

"Er ..." I began.

I thought about lying to her. Something stopped me. And that was the best thing I'd done in months.

"I got beaten up by a lad called Mitesh," I told her. The truth.

She nodded.

"Isn't he the brother of that girl – Neeta?" she asked. It wasn't really a question. She already knew everything.

I gave a shrug. It felt like that was all I ever did.

"Yeah," I said, softly. "You know about it, don't you?"

"Yes," she told me.

"Since when?" I asked.

Kelly looked away as she spoke.

"Your mate told me. Jag or whatever his name is," she replied.

"*Jag?*"

"Yeah – he came round last Sunday and told me. After Rachel's party," she said.

101

"Oh." I didn't know what else to say.

"Why didn't you tell me when I asked you out?" she asked.

"I dunno," I told her. "I was so excited that you'd asked me and I just ..."

"Just *what*?" she replied. She was starting to look angry.

"I dunno," I said again. "There's no excuse."

"Did you know that your mate was seeing Neeta too?" she told me.

"I found out today," I had to say.

"Serves you right, if you ask me," she said.

"I know," I muttered.

Kelly looked into my eyes before she said anything else.

"I'm going back inside now," she said.

"Why ain't you at school?" I asked.

"Because all my mates know that you were two-timing me and I'm embarrassed," she said at last.

"Oh."

I was waiting for her to tell me that she was dumping me. She didn't.

"You look like you need some painkillers," she told me.

"Yeah – I'm just on my way home," I replied.

"Why don't you come in first?" she said to me.

She must have seen the look of shock on my face. I had been waiting for her to swear at me or hit me. But she just stood there, looking upset for me. I'll be honest. I nearly started to cry. That was when I knew how stupid I'd been.

"You *really* want *me* to come in?" I asked.

She nodded.

"But I want you to tell me the truth. All of it."

"OK," I said. I didn't feel great but I was already feeling much better than I had for days.

"And if you lie to me again – I'm gonna kill you," Kelly told me. Her eyes looked as if they were on fire. I believed her.

****

It took a few months for the two-timer jokes to stop. For a few weeks everyone at school kept away from me. But, in the end, they all forgot about it. Jag and Neeta split up after about a month. Neeta told Jag that he wasn't rich enough to go out with her. Simple as that.

In the end I forgave him too and we all went back to being mates. Marcus still jokes about it, now and then, but he's like that. And his jokes are lame.

As for Kelly, she was a bit off with me for a while, which I didn't mind. It's not like I could complain about it. Not after what I'd done to her. I was lucky that she stayed with me. We're still together now. She makes jokes about what I did. When we're alone, she calls me two-timer. But I've learnt my lesson. I'm never getting into two-timing again. As long as I live. It just ain't worth it.

Barrington Stoke would like to thank all its readers for commenting on the manuscript before publication and in particular:

Amber Adseh
Lizzie Alder
Monjur Ali
Zora Amin
Dayne Liam Argyle
Lizzie Astles
Sampreet Bagri
Della Bartram
Shabana Begum
Tariq Boodhoo
Alana Butler
Michelle Byrne
Sanjay Champaneri
Manil Chauhan
Chandi Chavda
Bella Chohoun
Usha Chudasama
Vanisha Chudesama
Raeesa Chunara
Tadia Clarke
Kevindra Dajee
Monisha Dajee
Samantha Darby
Amrit Doll
Betty Elliott
Anam Fayyaz
Adam Gallagher
Gurneet Gill
Poonam Gohil

Paul Goss
Natasha Griffin
Amit K Hansrani
Josh Harper
Kimberley Harper
Ricky Harsum
Alistair Hay
Henel Joshi
Timmy Joyner
Sarbit Kaur Kainm
Jasuir Kainth
Saesta Kasmani
Rawinda Kaur
Jenny King
Rachael Lavender
Shama Mandhill
Farhana Meah
Sophie Melville
Rabiroon Miah
Nathan Morgan
Salma Moulvi
Leesha Muman
Nicky Mustoe
Hannah Naylor
Emily Norman
Marijana Novak
Helen Pallett
Mayuri Parmar
Aarti Patel

Aisha Patel
Ashish Patel
Mira Patel
Roslini Patel
Urvashi Patel
Jade Louise Pearson
Kayleigh Picton
Sarah Playfair
Bhagwant Kaur Punia
Jahira Ravat
Sinead Robinson
Harman Sahota
Lisa Shah
Ayesha Sharda
Grace Sharpe
Francis Louise Shelley
Phylicia Simon
Kinnan Solanki
Abbie-Louise Stokes
Dexter Stone
Kyle Swaby
Gareth Templeman
Eakta Thobhani
Jemini Vyas
Neha Vyas
Charlotte Waldron
Alison Willing
Eibhlin Zeal

Become a Consultant!

Would you like to give us feedback on our titles before they are published? Contact us at the email address below – we'd love to hear from you!

info@barringtonstoke.co.uk
www.barringtonstoke.co.uk